Contents

Foreword

The National Curriculum lies at the heart of our policies to raise standards. It sets out a clear, full and statutory entitlement to learning for all pupils. It determines the content of what will be taught, and sets attainment targets for learning. It also determines how performance will be assessed and reported. An effective National Curriculum therefore gives teachers, pupils, parents, employers and their wider community a clear and shared understanding of the skills and knowledge that young people will gain at school. It allows schools to meet the individual learning needs of pupils and to develop a distinctive character and ethos rooted in their local communities. And it provides a framework within which all partners in education can support young people on the road to further learning.

Getting the National Curriculum right presents difficult choices and balances. It must be robust enough to define and defend the core of knowledge and cultural experience which is the entitlement of every pupil, and at the same time flexible enough to give teachers the scope to build their teaching around it in ways which will enhance its delivery to their pupils.

The focus of this National Curriculum, together with the wider school curriculum, is therefore to ensure that pupils develop from an early age the essential literacy and numeracy skills they need to learn; to provide them with a guaranteed, full and rounded entitlement to learning; to foster their creativity; and to give teachers discretion to find the best ways to inspire in their pupils a joy and commitment to learning that will last a lifetime.

An entitlement to learning must be an entitlement for all pupils. This National Curriculum includes for the first time a detailed, overarching statement on inclusion which makes clear the principles schools must follow in their teaching right across the curriculum, to ensure that all pupils have the chance to succeed, whatever their individual needs and the potential barriers to their learning may be.

Equality of opportunity is one of a broad set of common values and purposes which underpin the school curriculum and the work of schools. These also include a commitment to valuing ourselves, our families and other relationships, the wider groups to which we belong, the diversity in our society and the environment in which we live. Until now, ours was one of the few national curricula not to have a statement of rationale setting out the fundamental principles underlying the curriculum. The handbooks for primary and secondary teachers include for the first time such a statement.

This is also the first National Curriculum in England to include citizenship, from September 2002, as part of the statutory curriculum for secondary schools. Education in citizenship and democracy will provide coherence in the way in which all pupils are helped to develop a full understanding of their roles and responsibilities as citizens in a modern democracy. It will play an important role, alongside other aspects of the curriculum and school life, in helping pupils to deal with difficult moral and social questions that arise in their lives and in society. The handbooks also provide for the first time a national framework for the teaching of personal, social and health education. Both elements reflect the fact that education is also about helping pupils to develop the knowledge, skills and understanding they need to live confident, healthy, independent lives, as individuals, parents, workers and members of society.

Rt Hon David Blunkett
Secretary of State for Education
and Employment

Sir William Stubbs
Chairman, Qualifications
and Curriculum Authority

About this booklet

This booklet:

- sets out the legal requirements of the National Curriculum in England for art and design
- provides information to help teachers implement art and design in their schools.

It has been written for coordinators, subject leaders and those who teach art and design, and is one of a series of separate booklets for each National Curriculum subject.

The National Curriculum for pupils aged five to 11 is set out in the handbook for primary teachers. The National Curriculum for pupils aged 11 to 16 is set out in the handbook for secondary teachers.

All these publications, and materials that support the teaching, learning and assessment of art and design, can be found on the National Curriculum web site at www.nc.uk.net.

About art and design in the National Curriculum

The structure of the National Curriculum

The programmes of study[1] set out what pupils should be taught, and the attainment target sets out the expected standards of pupils' performance. It is for schools to choose how they organise their school curriculum to include the programmes of study for art and design.

The programmes of study

The programmes of study set out what pupils should be taught in art and design at key stages 1, 2, and 3 and provide the basis for planning schemes of work. When planning, schools should also consider the general teaching requirements for inclusion, use of language, use of information and communication technology, and health and safety that apply across the programmes of study.

The **Knowledge, skills and understanding** in the programmes of study identify the aspects of art and design in which pupils make progress:

- exploring and developing ideas
- investigating and making art, craft and design
- evaluating and developing work
- developing knowledge and understanding.

Teaching should ensure that investigating and making includes exploring and developing ideas and evaluating and developing work. Knowledge and understanding should inform this process.

These aspects of art and design are developed through individual and collaborative work in two and three dimensions and on different scales, using a range of materials and processes, and through investigating the work of artists, craftspeople and designers as set out in **Breadth of study**.

Schools may find the DfEE/QCA exemplar schemes of work at key stages 1, 2 and 3 helpful to show how the programmes of study and attainment target can be translated into practical, manageable teaching plans.

[1] The Education Act 1996, section 353b, defines a programme of study as the 'matters, skills and processes' that should be taught to pupils of different abilities and maturities during the key stage.

Attainment target and level descriptions

The attainment target for art and design sets out the 'knowledge, skills and understanding that pupils of different abilities and maturities are expected to have by the end of each key stage'[2]. The attainment target consists of eight level descriptions of increasing difficulty, plus a description for exceptional performance above level 8. Each level description describes the types and range of performance that pupils working at that level should characteristically demonstrate.

In art and design, the level descriptions indicate progression in exploring and developing ideas, investigating and making art, craft and design and evaluating and developing work. Knowledge and understanding supports attainment in all three aspects.

The level descriptions provide the basis on which to make judgements about pupils' performance at the end of key stages 1, 2 and 3. At key stage 4, national qualifications are the main means of assessing attainment in art and design.

Range of levels within which the great majority of pupils are expected to work		Expected attainment for the majority of pupils at the end of the key stage	
Key stage 1	**1–3**	at age 7	**2**
Key stage 2	**2–5**	at age 11	**4**
Key stage 3	**3–7**	at age 14	**5/6**

Assessing attainment at the end of a key stage

In deciding on a pupil's level of attainment at the end of a key stage, teachers should judge which description best fits the pupil's performance. When doing so, each description should be considered alongside descriptions for adjacent levels.

Arrangements for statutory assessment at the end of each key stage are set out in detail in QCA's annual booklets about assessment and reporting arrangements.

[2] As defined by the Education Act 1996, section 353a.

Learning across the National Curriculum

The importance of art and design to pupils' education is set out on page 14. The handbooks for primary and secondary teachers also set out in general terms how the National Curriculum can promote learning across the curriculum in a number of areas such as spiritual, moral, social and cultural development, key skills and thinking skills. The examples below indicate specific ways in which the teaching of art and design can contribute to learning across the curriculum.

Promoting pupils' spiritual, moral, social and cultural development through art and design

For example, art and design provides opportunities to promote:

- *spiritual development,* through helping pupils to explore ideas, feelings and meanings and to make sense of them in a personal way in their own creative work, and to make connections with the experiences of others, as represented in works of art, craft and design
- *moral development,* through helping pupils to identify and discuss how artists, craftspeople and designers represent moral issues in their work [for example, Picasso's condemnation of warfare in his painting *Guernica*]
- *social development,* through helping pupils to learn to value different ideas and contributions and develop respect for the ideas and opinions of others, and to work on collaborative projects, making the most of different strengths and interests within a team
- *cultural development,* through helping pupils to recognise how images and artefacts can have an influence on the way people think and feel, and to understand the ideas, beliefs and values behind their making, relating art, craft and design to its cultural context [for example, the use of icons in religious art, and corporate advertising].

Promoting key skills through art and design

For example, art and design provides opportunities for pupils to develop the key skills of:

- *communication,* through exploring and recording ideas, discussing starting points and source materials for their work, finding out about art, craft and design using appropriate sources of information, and evaluating their own and others' work
- *application of number,* through understanding and using patterns and properties of shape in visualising and making images and artefacts, working in two and three dimensions and on different scales, understanding and using the properties of position and movement [for example, rotating and transforming shapes for a repeat pattern], and scaling up a preparatory drawing for a large-scale painting
- *IT,* through developing and recording ideas [for example, in an electronic sketchbook], using the internet to investigate the work of artists, craftspeople and designers, using IT to extend and enhance their use of materials and processes, exchanging work and ideas using e-mail, and developing their own class art gallery as a web site

- *working with others,* through collaborating on projects, working in two and three dimensions and on different scales [for example, working in a group and negotiating ideas and tasks]; and meeting a design brief
- *improving pupils' own learning and performance,* through discussing and critically questioning visual and other information, including the starting points for their work; and reflecting on and evaluating their own and others' work and planning ways to develop their own work further
- *problem solving,* through manipulating materials, processes and technologies, responding, experimenting, adapting their thinking and arriving at diverse solutions, synthesising observations, ideas, feelings and meanings, and designing and making art, craft and design.

Promoting other aspects of the curriculum

For example, art and design provides opportunities to promote:

- *thinking skills,* through encouraging pupils to ask and answer questions about starting points for their work, explore and develop ideas, collect and organise visual and other information and use this to develop their work, investigate possibilities, review what they have done, adapt or refine their work, and make reasoned judgements and decisions about how to develop their ideas
- *enterprise and entrepreneurial skills,* through developing pupils' willingness to explore and consider alternative ideas, views and possibilities, developing characteristics such as being prepared to take risks and to persevere when things go wrong, and encouraging pupils to be creative and imaginative, to innovate, to use their intuition and to develop self-confidence and independence of mind
- *work-related learning,* through broadening pupils' understanding of what an artist, craftsperson or designer is or does [for example, by visiting a practising craftperson's workshop]; developing pupils' understanding of the relevance of the art and design curriculum to what artists, craftspeople and designers do in their work [for example by carrying out a design brief that has a commercial context], developing pupils' knowledge and understanding of the diverse roles and functions of art, craft and design in contemporary life; and helping pupils recognise the range of possibilities for employment in the creative and cultural industries
- *education for sustainable development,* through developing pupils' knowledge and understanding of the role of art and design in shaping sustainable environments, and exploring values and ethics within art and design.

The programmes of study
for art and design

A common structure and design for all subjects

The programmes of study

The National Curriculum programmes of study have been given a common structure and a common design.

In each subject, at each key stage, the main column **1** contains the programme of study, which sets out two sorts of requirements:

- **Knowledge, skills and understanding 2** – what has to be taught in the subject during the key stage
- **Breadth of study 3** – the contexts, activities, areas of study and range of experiences through which the **Knowledge, skills and understanding** should be taught.

Schools are not required by law to teach the content in grey type. This includes the examples in the main column **4** [printed inside square brackets], all text in the margins **5** and information and examples in the inclusion statement.

The programmes of study for English, mathematics and science

The programmes of study for English and science contain sections that correspond directly to the attainment targets for each subject. In mathematics this one-to-one correspondence does not hold for all key stages – see the mathematics programme of study for more information. In English, the three sections of the programme of study each contain **Breadth of study** requirements. In mathematics and science there is a single, separate set of **Breadth of study** requirements for each key stage.

The programmes of study in the non-core foundation subjects

In these subjects (except for citizenship) the programme of study simply contains two sets of requirements – **Knowledge, skills and understanding** and **Breadth of study**. The programmes of study for citizenship contain no **Breadth of study** requirements.

Information in the margins

At the start of each key stage, the margin begins with a summary **6** of the main things that pupils will learn during the key stage. The margins also contain four other types of non-statutory information:

- notes giving key information that should be taken into account when teaching the subject
- notes giving definitions of words and phrases in the programmes of study
- suggested opportunities for pupils to use information and communication technology (ICT) as they learn the subject
- some key links with other subjects indicating connections between teaching requirements, and suggesting how a requirement in one subject can build on the requirements in another in the same key stage.

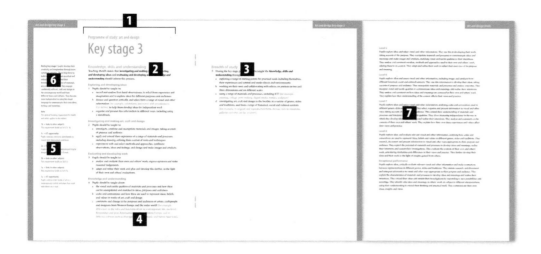

The referencing system

References work as follows:

A reference in ...	... reads ...	... and means ...
Physical education key stage 2	11a, 11b → links to other subjects These requirements build on Gg/2c.	Physical education key stage 2, requirements 11a and 11b build on geography (key stage 2), paragraph 2, requirement c.
Art and design key stage 1	4a → links to other subjects This requirement builds on Ma3/2a, 2c, 2d.	Art and design key stage 1, requirement 4a builds on mathematics (key stage 1), Ma3 Shape, space and measures, paragraph 2, requirements a, c and d.
Citizenship key stage 3	1a → links to other subjects This requirement builds on Hi/10, 13.	Citizenship key stage 3, requirement 1a builds on history (key stage 3) paragraphs 10 and 13.

The attainment target

The attainment target **7** is at the end of this booklet. It can be read alongside the programmes of study by folding out the flap.

Art and design is the freedom of the individual, the freedom of expression and the freedom to fail without retort.

Simon Waterfall, Creative Director, Deepend

Art develops spiritual values and contributes a wider understanding to the experience of life, which helps to build a balanced personality.

Bridget Riley, Painter

Art and design is not just a subject to learn, but an activity that you can practise: with your hands, your eyes, your whole personality.

Quentin Blake, Children's Laureate

Awareness and interaction with design is part of the contemporary professional environment. Design issues enter our life every day.

Peter Saville, Art Director and Designer

The importance of art and design*
Art and design stimulates creativity and imagination. It provides visual, tactile and sensory experiences and a unique way of understanding and responding to the world. Pupils use colour, form, texture, pattern and different materials and processes to communicate what they see, feel and think. Through art and design activities, they learn to make informed value judgements and aesthetic and practical decisions, becoming actively involved in shaping environments. They explore ideas and meanings in the work of artists, craftspeople and designers. They learn about the diverse roles and functions of art, craft and design in contemporary life, and in different times and cultures. Understanding, appreciation and enjoyment of the visual arts have the power to enrich our personal and public lives.
* Art and design includes craft.

Programme of study: art and design

Key stage 1

During key stage 1 pupils develop their creativity and imagination by exploring the visual, tactile and sensory qualities of materials and processes. They learn about the role of art, craft and design in their environment. They begin to understand colour, shape and space and pattern and texture and use them to represent their ideas and feelings.

Note
The general teaching requirement for health and safety applies in this subject.

1b → links to other subjects
This requirement builds on En1/2c, 2d, 3d.

2b → links to other subjects
This requirement builds on D&T/2c.

3a → links to other subjects
This requirement builds on En1/3c, 3d.

4a → links to other subjects
This requirement builds on Ma3/2a, 2c, 2d.

4a → ICT opportunity
Pupils could use 'paint' software to explore shape, colour and pattern.

Knowledge, skills and understanding

Teaching should ensure that **investigating and making** includes **exploring and developing ideas** and **evaluating and developing work**. **Knowledge and understanding** should inform this process.

Exploring and developing ideas

1   Pupils should be taught to:
   a   record from first-hand observation, experience and imagination, and explore ideas
   b   ask and answer questions about the starting points for their work, and develop their ideas.

Investigating and making art, craft and design

2   Pupils should be taught to:
   a   investigate the possibilities of a range of materials and processes
   b   try out tools and techniques and apply these to materials and processes, including drawing
   c   represent observations, ideas and feelings, and design and make images and artefacts.

Evaluating and developing work

3   Pupils should be taught to:
   a   review what they and others have done and say what they think and feel about it
   b   identify what they might change in their current work or develop in their future work.

Knowledge and understanding

4   Pupils should be taught about:
   a   visual and tactile elements, including colour, pattern and texture, line and tone, shape, form and space
   b   materials and processes used in making art, craft and design
   c   differences and similarities in the work of artists, craftspeople and designers in different times and cultures [for example, sculptors, photographers, architects, textile designers].

Breadth of study

5   During the key stage, pupils should be taught the **Knowledge, skills and understanding** through:

a   exploring a range of starting points for practical work [for example, themselves, their experiences, stories, natural and made objects and the local environment]

b   working on their own, and collaborating with others, on projects in two and three dimensions and on different scales

c   using a range of materials and processes [for example, painting, collage, print making, digital media, textiles, sculpture]

d   investigating different kinds of art, craft and design [for example, in the locality, in original and reproduction form, during visits to museums, galleries and sites, on the internet].

Key stage 2

During key stage 2 pupils develop their creativity and imagination through more complex activities. These help to build on their skills and improve their control of materials, tools and techniques. They increase their critical awareness of the roles and purposes of art, craft and design in different times and cultures. They become more confident in using visual and tactile elements and materials and processes to communicate what they see, feel and think.

Note
The general teaching requirement for health and safety applies in this subject.

1b → links to other subjects
This requirement builds on En1/2b, 2e.

1c → ICT opportunity
Pupils could use digital and video cameras to record observations.

2b → links to other subjects
This requirement builds on D&T/2d.

2b → ICT opportunity
Pupils could use digital images as a starting point for creative textile work.

3a → links to other subjects
This requirement builds on En1/3b, 3c.

3a → ICT opportunity
Pupils could develop their own class art gallery on the school web site.

4a → links to other subjects
This requirement builds on Ma3/2d, 3b.

Knowledge, skills and understanding

Teaching should ensure that **investigating and making** includes **exploring and developing ideas** and **evaluating and developing work. Knowledge and understanding** should inform this process.

Exploring and developing ideas

1 Pupils should be taught to:

a record from experience and imagination, to select and record from first-hand observation and to explore ideas for different purposes

b question and make thoughtful observations about starting points and select ideas to use in their work

c collect visual and other information [for example, images, materials] to help them develop their ideas, including using a sketchbook.

Investigating and making art, craft and design

2 Pupils should be taught to:

a investigate and combine visual and tactile qualities of materials and processes and to match these qualities to the purpose of the work

b apply their experience of materials and processes, including drawing, developing their control of tools and techniques

c use a variety of methods and approaches to communicate observations, ideas and feelings, and to design and make images and artefacts.

Evaluating and developing work

3 Pupils should be taught to:

a compare ideas, methods and approaches in their own and others' work and say what they think and feel about them

b adapt their work according to their views and describe how they might develop it further.

Knowledge and understanding

4 Pupils should be taught about:

a visual and tactile elements, including colour, pattern and texture, line and tone, shape, form and space, and how these elements can be combined and organised for different purposes

b materials and processes used in art, craft and design and how these can be matched to ideas and intentions

c the roles and purposes of artists, craftspeople and designers working in different times and cultures [for example, Western Europe and the wider world].

Breadth of study

5   During the key stage, pupils should be taught the **Knowledge, skills and understanding** through:

a   exploring a range of starting points for practical work [for example, themselves, their experiences, images, stories, drama, music, natural and made objects and environments]

b   working on their own, and collaborating with others, on projects in two and three dimensions and on different scales

c   using a range of materials and processes, including ICT [for example, painting, collage, print making, digital media, textiles, sculpture]

d   investigating art, craft and design in the locality and in a variety of genres, styles and traditions [for example, in original and reproduction form, during visits to museums, galleries and sites, on the internet].

Programme of study: art and design

Key stage 3

During key stage 3 pupils develop their creativity and imagination through more sustained activities. These help them to build on and improve their practical and critical skills and to extend their knowledge and experience of materials, processes and practices. They engage confidently with art, craft and design in the contemporary world and from different times and cultures. They become more independent in using the visual language to communicate their own ideas, feelings and meanings.

Knowledge, skills and understanding

Teaching should ensure that **investigating and making** includes **exploring and developing ideas** and **evaluating and developing work**. **Knowledge and understanding** should inform this process.

Exploring and developing ideas

1   Pupils should be taught to:
   a   record and analyse first-hand observations, to select from experience and imagination and to explore ideas for different purposes and audiences
   b   discuss and question critically, and select from a range of visual and other information [for example, exhibitions, interviews with practitioners, CD-ROMs] to help them develop ideas for independent work
   c   organise and present this information in different ways, including using a sketchbook.

Investigating and making art, craft and design

2   Pupils should be taught to:
   a   investigate, combine and manipulate materials and images, taking account of purpose and audience
   b   apply and extend their experience of a range of materials and processes, including drawing, refining their control of tools and techniques
   c   experiment with and select methods and approaches, synthesise observations, ideas and feelings, and design and make images and artefacts.

Evaluating and developing work

3   Pupils should be taught to:
   a   analyse and evaluate their own and others' work, express opinions and make reasoned judgements
   b   adapt and refine their work and plan and develop this further, in the light of their own and others' evaluations.

Knowledge and understanding

4   Pupils should be taught about:
   a   the visual and tactile qualities of materials and processes and how these can be manipulated and matched to ideas, purposes and audiences
   b   codes and conventions and how these are used to represent ideas, beliefs, and values in works of art, craft and design
   c   continuity and change in the purposes and audiences of artists, craftspeople and designers from Western Europe and the wider world [for example, differences in the roles and functions of art in contemporary life, medieval, Renaissance and post-Renaissance periods in Western Europe, and in different cultures such as Aboriginal, African, Islamic and Native American].

Note
The general teaching requirement for health and safety applies in this subject.

1b → links to other subjects
This requirement builds on En1/2f, 3b.

1c → ICT opportunity
Pupils could use electronic sketchbooks to record their observations and ideas.

2a → ICT opportunity
Pupils could manipulate and interpret digital images to create 2-D and 3-D work.

2b → links to other subjects
This requirement builds on D&T/2c.

3a → links to other subjects
This requirement builds on En1/3e.

3a → ICT opportunity
Pupils could recreate works of art in a contemporary context and share their work with others via e-mail.

Breadth of study

5   During the key stage, pupils should be taught the **Knowledge, skills and understanding** through:

a   exploring a range of starting points for practical work including themselves, their experiences and natural and made objects and environments

b   working on their own, and collaborating with others, on projects in two and three dimensions and on different scales

c   using a range of materials and processes, including ICT [for example, painting, collage, print making, digital media, textiles, sculpture]

d   investigating art, craft and design in the locality, in a variety of genres, styles and traditions, and from a range of historical, social and cultural contexts [for example, in original and reproduction form, during visits to museums, galleries and sites, on the internet].

General teaching requirements

Inclusion: providing effective learning opportunities for all pupils

Schools have a responsibility to provide a broad and balanced curriculum for all pupils. The National Curriculum is the starting point for planning a school curriculum that meets the specific needs of individuals and groups of pupils. This statutory inclusion statement on providing effective learning opportunities for all pupils outlines how teachers can modify, as necessary, the National Curriculum programmes of study to provide all pupils with relevant and appropriately challenging work at each key stage. It sets out three principles that are essential to developing a more inclusive curriculum:

A Setting suitable learning challenges

B Responding to pupils' diverse learning needs

C Overcoming potential barriers to learning and assessment for individuals and groups of pupils.

Applying these principles should keep to a minimum the need for aspects of the National Curriculum to be disapplied for a pupil.

Schools are able to provide other curricular opportunities outside the National Curriculum to meet the needs of individuals or groups of pupils such as speech and language therapy and mobility training.

Three principles for inclusion

In planning and teaching the National Curriculum, teachers are required to have due regard to the following principles.

A Setting suitable learning challenges

1   Teachers should aim to give every pupil the opportunity to experience success in learning and to achieve as high a standard as possible. The National Curriculum programmes of study set out what most pupils should be taught at each key stage – but teachers should teach the knowledge, skills and understanding in ways that suit their pupils' abilities. This may mean choosing knowledge, skills and understanding from earlier or later key stages so that individual pupils can make progress and show what they can achieve. Where it is appropriate for pupils to make extensive use of content from an earlier key stage, there may not be time to teach all aspects of the age-related programmes of study. A similarly flexible approach will be needed to take account of any gaps in pupils' learning resulting from missed or interrupted schooling [for example, that may be experienced by travellers, refugees, those in care or those with long-term medical conditions, including pupils with neurological problems, such as head injuries, and those with degenerative conditions].

2   For pupils whose attainments fall significantly below the expected levels at a particular key stage, a much greater degree of differentiation will be necessary. In these circumstances, teachers may need to use the content of the programmes of study as a resource or to provide a context, in planning learning appropriate to the age and requirements of their pupils.[1]

3   For pupils whose attainments significantly exceed the expected level of attainment within one or more subjects during a particular key stage, teachers will need to plan suitably challenging work. As well as drawing on materials from later key stages or higher levels of study, teachers may plan further differentiation by extending the breadth and depth of study within individual subjects or by planning work which draws on the content of different subjects.[2]

B   Responding to pupils' diverse learning needs

1   When planning, teachers should set high expectations and provide opportunities for all pupils to achieve, including boys and girls, pupils with special educational needs, pupils with disabilities, pupils from all social and cultural backgrounds, pupils of different ethnic groups including travellers, refugees and asylum seekers, and those from diverse linguistic backgrounds. Teachers need to be aware that pupils bring to school different experiences, interests and strengths which will influence the way in which they learn. Teachers should plan their approaches to teaching and learning so that all pupils can take part in lessons fully and effectively.

2   To ensure that they meet the full range of pupils' needs, teachers should be aware of the requirements of the equal opportunities legislation that covers race, gender and disability.[3]

3   Teachers should take specific action to respond to pupils' diverse needs by:
  a   creating effective learning environments
  b   securing their motivation and concentration
  c   providing equality of opportunity through teaching approaches
  d   using appropriate assessment approaches
  e   setting targets for learning.

Examples for B/3a – creating effective learning environments
Teachers create effective learning environments in which:
- the contribution of all pupils is valued
- all pupils can feel secure and are able to contribute appropriately
- stereotypical views are challenged and pupils learn to appreciate and view positively differences in others, whether arising from race, gender, ability or disability

---

[1] Teachers may find QCA's guidance on planning work for pupils with learning difficulties a helpful companion to the programmes of study.
[2] Teachers may find QCA's guidance on meeting the requirements of gifted and talented pupils a helpful companion to the programmes of study.
[3] The Sex Discrimination Act 1975, the Race Relations Act 1976, the Disability Discrimination Act 1995.

- pupils learn to take responsibility for their actions and behaviours both in school and in the wider community
- all forms of bullying and harassment, including racial harassment, are challenged
- pupils are enabled to participate safely in clothing appropriate to their religious beliefs, particularly in subjects such as science, design and technology and physical education.

Examples for B/3b – securing motivation and concentration
Teachers secure pupils' motivation and concentration by:

- using teaching approaches appropriate to different learning styles
- using, where appropriate, a range of organisational approaches, such as setting, grouping or individual work, to ensure that learning needs are properly addressed
- varying subject content and presentation so that this matches their learning needs
- planning work which builds on their interests and cultural experiences
- planning appropriately challenging work for those whose ability and understanding are in advance of their language skills
- using materials which reflect social and cultural diversity and provide positive images of race, gender and disability
- planning and monitoring the pace of work so that they all have a chance to learn effectively and achieve success
- taking action to maintain interest and continuity of learning for pupils who may be absent for extended periods of time.

Examples for B/3c – providing equality of opportunity
Teaching approaches that provide equality of opportunity include:

- ensuring that boys and girls are able to participate in the same curriculum, particularly in science, design and technology and physical education
- taking account of the interests and concerns of boys and girls by using a range of activities and contexts for work and allowing a variety of interpretations and outcomes, particularly in English, science, design and technology, ICT, art and design, music and physical education
- avoiding gender stereotyping when organising pupils into groups, assigning them to activities or arranging access to equipment, particularly in science, design and technology, ICT, music and physical education
- taking account of pupils' specific religious or cultural beliefs relating to the representation of ideas or experiences or to the use of particular types of equipment, particularly in science, design and technology, ICT and art and design
- enabling the fullest possible participation of pupils with disabilities or particular medical needs in all subjects, offering positive role models and making provision, where necessary, to facilitate access to activities with appropriate support, aids or adaptations. (See **Overcoming potential barriers to learning and assessment for individuals and groups of pupils**.)

Examples for B/3d – using appropriate assessment approaches

Teachers use appropriate assessment approaches that:

- allow for different learning styles and ensure that pupils are given the chance and encouragement to demonstrate their competence and attainment through appropriate means
- are familiar to the pupils and for which they have been adequately prepared
- use materials which are free from discrimination and stereotyping in any form
- provide clear and unambiguous feedback to pupils to aid further learning.

Examples for B/3e – setting targets for learning

Teachers set targets for learning that:

- build on pupils' knowledge, experiences, interests and strengths to improve areas of weakness and demonstrate progression over time
- are attainable and yet challenging and help pupils to develop their self-esteem and confidence in their ability to learn.

C Overcoming potential barriers to learning and assessment for individuals and groups of pupils

A minority of pupils will have particular learning and assessment requirements which go beyond the provisions described in sections A and B and, if not addressed, could create barriers to learning. These requirements are likely to arise as a consequence of a pupil having a special educational need or disability or may be linked to a pupil's progress in learning English as an additional language.

1   Teachers must take account of these requirements and make provision, where necessary, to support individuals or groups of pupils to enable them to participate effectively in the curriculum and assessment activities. During end of key stage assessments, teachers should bear in mind that special arrangements are available to support individual pupils.

Pupils with special educational needs

2   Curriculum planning and assessment for pupils with special educational needs must take account of the type and extent of the difficulty experienced by the pupil. Teachers will encounter a wide range of pupils with special educational needs, some of whom will also have disabilities (see paragraphs C/4 and C/5). In many cases, the action necessary to respond to an individual's requirements for curriculum access will be met through greater differentiation of tasks and materials, consistent with school-based intervention as set out in the SEN Code of Practice. A smaller number of pupils may need access to specialist equipment and approaches or to alternative or adapted activities, consistent with school-based intervention augmented by advice and support from external specialists as described in the SEN Code of Practice, or, in exceptional circumstances, with a statement of special educational need.

Teachers should, where appropriate, work closely with representatives of other agencies who may be supporting the pupil.

3   Teachers should take specific action to provide access to learning for pupils with special educational needs by:

   a   providing for pupils who need help with communication, language and literacy

   b   planning, where necessary, to develop pupils' understanding through the use of all available senses and experiences

   c   planning for pupils' full participation in learning and in physical and practical activities

   d   helping pupils to manage their behaviour, to take part in learning effectively and safely, and, at key stage 4, to prepare for work

   e   helping individuals to manage their emotions, particularly trauma or stress, and to take part in learning.

Examples for C/3a – helping with communication, language and literacy
Teachers provide for pupils who need help with communication, language and literacy through:

- using texts that pupils can read and understand
- using visual and written materials in different formats, including large print, symbol text and Braille
- using ICT, other technological aids and taped materials
- using alternative and augmentative communication, including signs and symbols
- using translators, communicators and amanuenses.

Examples for C/3b – developing understanding
Teachers develop pupils' understanding through the use of all available senses and experiences, by:

- using materials and resources that pupils can access through sight, touch, sound, taste or smell
- using word descriptions and other stimuli to make up for a lack of first-hand experiences
- using ICT, visual and other materials to increase pupils' knowledge of the wider world
- encouraging pupils to take part in everyday activities such as play, drama, class visits and exploring the environment.

Examples for C/3c – planning for full participation
Teachers plan for pupils' full participation in learning and in physical and practical activities through:

- using specialist aids and equipment
- providing support from adults or peers when needed
- adapting tasks or environments
- providing alternative activities, where necessary.

Examples for C/3d – managing behaviour
Teachers help pupils to manage their behaviour, take part in learning
effectively and safely, and, at key stage 4, prepare for work by:
- setting realistic demands and stating them explicitly
- using positive behaviour management, including a clear structure
  of rewards and sanctions
- giving pupils every chance and encouragement to develop the skills
  they need to work well with a partner or a group
- teaching pupils to value and respect the contribution of others
- encouraging and teaching independent working skills
- teaching essential safety rules.

Examples for C/3e – managing emotions
Teachers help individuals manage their emotions and take part
in learning through:
- identifying aspects of learning in which the pupil will engage and
  plan short-term, easily achievable goals in selected activities
- providing positive feedback to reinforce and encourage learning and
  build self-esteem
- selecting tasks and materials sensitively to avoid unnecessary stress
  for the pupil
- creating a supportive learning environment in which the pupil feels
  safe and is able to engage with learning
- allowing time for the pupil to engage with learning and gradually
  increasing the range of activities and demands.

Pupils with disabilities

4   Not all pupils with disabilities will necessarily have special educational needs.
    Many pupils with disabilities learn alongside their peers with little need for
    additional resources beyond the aids which they use as part of their daily life,
    such as a wheelchair, a hearing aid or equipment to aid vision. Teachers must
    take action, however, in their planning to ensure that these pupils are enabled
    to participate as fully and effectively as possible within the National Curriculum
    and the statutory assessment arrangements. Potential areas of difficulty
    should be identified and addressed at the outset of work, without recourse
    to the formal provisions for disapplication.

5   Teachers should take specific action to enable the effective participation
    of pupils with disabilities by:
    a   planning appropriate amounts of time to allow for the satisfactory
        completion of tasks
    b   planning opportunities, where necessary, for the development of skills
        in practical aspects of the curriculum
    c   identifying aspects of programmes of study and attainment targets
        that may present specific difficulties for individuals.

Examples for C/5a – planning to complete tasks

Teachers plan appropriate amounts of time to allow pupils to complete tasks satisfactorily through:

- taking account of the very slow pace at which some pupils will be able to record work, either manually or with specialist equipment, and of the physical effort required
- being aware of the high levels of concentration necessary for some pupils when following or interpreting text or graphics, particularly when using vision aids or tactile methods, and of the tiredness which may result
- allocating sufficient time, opportunity and access to equipment for pupils to gain information through experimental work and detailed observation, including the use of microscopes
- being aware of the effort required by some pupils to follow oral work, whether through use of residual hearing, lip reading or a signer, and of the tiredness or loss of concentration which may occur.

Examples for C/5b – developing skills in practical aspects

Teachers create opportunities for the development of skills in practical aspects of the curriculum through:

- providing adapted, modified or alternative activities or approaches to learning in physical education and ensuring that these have integrity and equivalence to the National Curriculum and enable pupils to make appropriate progress
- providing alternative or adapted activities in science, art and design and design and technology for pupils who are unable to manipulate tools, equipment or materials or who may be allergic to certain types of materials
- ensuring that all pupils can be included and participate safely in geography fieldwork, local studies and visits to museums, historic buildings and sites.

Examples for C/5c – overcoming specific difficulties

Teachers overcome specific difficulties for individuals presented by aspects of the programmes of study and attainment targets through:

- using approaches to enable hearing impaired pupils to learn about sound in science and music
- helping visually impaired pupils to learn about light in science, to access maps and visual resources in geography and to evaluate different products in design and technology and images in art and design
- providing opportunities for pupils to develop strength in depth where they cannot meet the particular requirements of a subject, such as the visual requirements in art and design and the singing requirements in music
- discounting these aspects in appropriate individual cases when required to make a judgement against level descriptions.

Pupils who are learning English as an additional language

6 Pupils for whom English is an additional language have diverse needs in terms of support necessary in English language learning. Planning should take account of such factors as the pupil's age, length of time in this country, previous educational experience and skills in other languages. Careful monitoring of each pupil's progress in the acquisition of English language skills and of subject knowledge and understanding will be necessary to confirm that no learning difficulties are present.

7 The ability of pupils for whom English is an additional language to take part in the National Curriculum may be ahead of their communication skills in English. Teachers should plan learning opportunities to help pupils develop their English and should aim to provide the support pupils need to take part in all subject areas.

8 Teachers should take specific action to help pupils who are learning English as an additional language by:
   a developing their spoken and written English
   b ensuring access to the curriculum and to assessment.

Examples for C/8a – developing spoken and written English
Teachers develop pupils' spoken and written English through:
- ensuring that vocabulary work covers both the technical and everyday meaning of key words, metaphors and idioms
- explaining clearly how speaking and writing in English are structured to achieve different purposes, across a range of subjects
- providing a variety of reading material [for example, pupils' own work, the media, ICT, literature, reference books] that highlight the different ways English is used, especially those that help pupils to understand society and culture
- ensuring that there are effective opportunities for talk and that talk is used to support writing in all subjects
- where appropriate, encouraging pupils to transfer their knowledge, skills and understanding of one language to another, pointing out similarities and differences between languages
- building on pupils' experiences of language at home and in the wider community, so that their developing uses of English and other languages support one another.

Examples for C/8b – ensuring access
Teachers make sure pupils have access to the curriculum and to assessment through:
- using accessible texts and materials that suit pupils' ages and levels of learning
- providing support by using ICT or video or audio materials, dictionaries and translators, readers and amanuenses
- using home or first language, where appropriate.

Additional information for art and design

Teachers may find the following additional information helpful when implementing the statutory inclusion statement: **Providing effective learning opportunities for all pupils**. Teachers need to consider the full requirements of the inclusion statement when planning for individuals or groups of pupils. There are specific references to art and design in the examples for B/3c, C/5b and C/5c.

To overcome any potential barriers to learning in art and design, some pupils may require:

- alternative tasks to overcome any difficulties arising from specific religious beliefs relating to ideas and experiences they are expected to represent
- access to stimuli, participation in everyday events and explorations, materials, word descriptions and other resources, to compensate for a lack of specific first-hand experiences and to allow pupils to explore an idea or theme
- alternative or adapted activities to overcome difficulties with manipulating tools, equipment or materials
- help to manage particular types of materials to which they may be allergic.

In assessment:

- pupils who are visually impaired may be unable to complete the requirements of the programmes of study or attainment target relating to the visual aspects of art and design. Teachers should provide materials, equipment and resources for pupils to develop strength in depth by making a tactile response in practical and theoretical aspects of the subject. When a judgement against level descriptions is required, teachers should discount those aspects that relate to the visual aspects of art and design and use alternative, appropriate criteria in making judgements.

Use of language across the curriculum

1 Pupils should be taught in all subjects to express themselves correctly and appropriately and to read accurately and with understanding. Since standard English, spoken and written, is the predominant language in which knowledge and skills are taught and learned, pupils should be taught to recognise and use standard English.

Writing

2 In writing, pupils should be taught to use correct spelling and punctuation and follow grammatical conventions. They should also be taught to organise their writing in logical and coherent forms.

Speaking

3 In speaking, pupils should be taught to use language precisely and cogently.

Listening

4 Pupils should be taught to listen to others, and to respond and build on their ideas and views constructively.

Reading

5 In reading, pupils should be taught strategies to help them read with understanding, to locate and use information, to follow a process or argument and summarise, and to synthesise and adapt what they learn from their reading.

6 Pupils should be taught the technical and specialist vocabulary of subjects and how to use and spell these words. They should also be taught to use the patterns of language vital to understanding and expression in different subjects. These include the construction of sentences, paragraphs and texts that are often used in a subject [for example, language to express causality, chronology, logic, exploration, hypothesis, comparison, and how to ask questions and develop arguments]

Use of information and communication technology across the curriculum

1 Pupils should be given opportunities[1] to apply and develop their ICT capability through the use of ICT tools to support their learning in all subjects (with the exception of physical education at key stages 1 and 2).

2 Pupils should be given opportunities to support their work by being taught to:

a find things out from a variety of sources, selecting and synthesising the information to meet their needs and developing an ability to question its accuracy, bias and plausibility

b develop their ideas using ICT tools to amend and refine their work and enhance its quality and accuracy

c exchange and share information, both directly and through electronic media

d review, modify and evaluate their work, reflecting critically on its quality, as it progresses.

[1] At key stage 1, there are no statutory requirements to teach the use of ICT in the programmes of study for the non-core foundation subjects. Teachers should use their judgement to decide where it is appropriate to teach the use of ICT across these subjects at key stage 1. At other key stages, there are statutory requirements to use ICT in all subjects, except physical education.

Health and safety

1 This statement applies to science, design and technology, information and communication technology, art and design, and physical education.

2 When working with tools, equipment and materials, in practical activities and in different environments, including those that are unfamiliar, pupils should be taught:
   a about hazards, risks and risk control
   b to recognise hazards, assess consequent risks and take steps to control the risks to themselves and others
   c to use information to assess the immediate and cumulative risks
   d to manage their environment to ensure the health and safety of themselves and others
   e to explain the steps they take to control risks.

The attainment target
for art and design

About the attainment target

An attainment target sets out the 'knowledge, skills and understanding that pupils of different abilities and maturities are expected to have by the end of each key stage'[1]. Except in the case of citizenship[2], attainment targets consist of eight level descriptions of increasing difficulty, plus a description for exceptional performance above level 8. Each level description describes the types and range of performance that pupils working at that level should characteristically demonstrate.

The level descriptions provide the basis for making judgements about pupils' performance at the end of key stages 1, 2 and 3. At key stage 4, national qualifications are the main means of assessing attainment in art and design.

Range of levels within which the great majority of pupils are expected to work		Expected attainment for the majority of pupils at the end of the key stage	
Key stage 1	**1–3**	at age 7	**2**
Key stage 2	**2–5**	at age 11	**4**
Key stage 3	**3–7**	at age 14	**5/6**[3]

Assessing attainment at the end of a key stage

In deciding on a pupil's level of attainment at the end of a key stage, teachers should judge which description best fits the pupil's performance. When doing so, each description should be considered alongside descriptions for adjacent levels.

Arrangements for statutory assessment at the end of each key stage are set out in detail in QCA's annual booklets about assessment and reporting arrangements.

[1] As defined by the Education Act 1996, section 353a.
[2] In citizenship, expected performance for the majority of pupils at the end of key stages 3 and 4 is set out in end of key stage descriptions.
[3] Including modern foreign languages.

Acknowledgements

About the work used in this document
The artwork and photographs used in this book are the result of a national selection organised by QCA and the Design Council. We would like to thank all 3,108 pupils who took part and especially the following pupils and schools whose work has been used throughout the National Curriculum.

Pupils Frankie Allen, Sarah Anderson, Naomi Ball, Kristina Battleday, Ashley Boyle, Martin Broom, Katie Brown, Alex Bryant, Tania Burnett, Elizabeth Burrows, Caitie Calloway, Kavandeep Chahal, Donna Clarke, Leah Cliffe, Megan Coombs, Andrew Cornford, Samantha Davidoff, Jodie Evans, Holly Fowler, Rachel Fort, Christopher Fort, Hannah Foster, Ruth Fry, Nicholas Furlonge, Tasleem Ghanchi, Rebecca Goodwin, Megan Goodwin, Joanna Gray, Alisha Grazette, Emma Habbeshon, Zoe Hall, Kay Hampshire, Jessica Harris, Aimee Howard, Amy Hurst, Katherine Hymers, Safwan Ismael, Tamaszina Jacobs-Abiola, Tomi Johnson, Richard Jones, Bruno Jones, Thomas Kelleher, Sophie Lambert, Gareth Lloyd, Ope Majekodunmi, Sophie Manchester, Alex Massie, Amy McNair, Dale Meachen, Katherine Mills, Rebecca Moore, Andrew Morgan, Amber Murrell, Sally O'Connor, Rosie O'Reilly, Antonia Pain, Daniel Pamment, Jennie Plant, Christopher Prest, Megan Ramsay, Alice Ross, David Rowles, Amy Sandford, Zeba Saudagar, Nathan Scarfe, Daniel Scully, Bilal Shakoor, Sandeep Sharma, Morrad Siyahla, Daryl Smith, Catriona Statham, Scott Taylor, Amy Thornton, Jessica Tidmarsh, Alix Tinkler, Lucy Titford, Marion Tulloch, Charlotte Ward, Kaltuun Warsame, Emily Webb, Bradley West, Daniel Wilkinson, Soriah Williams, Susan Williamson, Helen Williamson, Charlotte Windmill, Ryan Wollan, Olivia Wright.

Schools Adam's Grammar School, Almondbury Junior School, Bishops Castle Community College, Bolton Brow Junior and Infant School, Boxford C of E Voluntary Controlled Primary School, Bugbrooke School, Cantell School, Charnwood Primary School, Cheselbourne County First School, Chester Catholic High School, Dales Infant School, Deanery C of E High School, Driffield C of E Infants' School, Dursley Primary School, Fourfields County Primary School, Furze Infants School, Gosforth High School, Grahame Park Junior School, Green Park Combined School, Gusford Community Primary School, Hartshill School, Headington School, Holyport Manor School, Jersey College for Girls Preparatory School, King Edward VI School, King James's School, Kingsway Junior School, Knutsford High School, Leiston Primary School, Maltby Manor Infant School, Mullion Comprehensive School, North Marston C of E First School, Norton Hill School, Penglais School, Priory Secondary School, Redknock School, Richard Whittington Primary School, Ringwood School, Sarah Bonnell School, Sedgemoor Manor Infants School, Selly Park Technology College for Girls, Southwark Infant School, St Albans High School for Girls, St Denys C of E Infant School, St Helen's C of E (Aided) Primary School, St John's Infants School, St Joseph's RC Infant School, St Laurence School, St Mary Magdalene School, St Matthews C of E Aided Primary School, St Michael's C of E School, St Saviour's and St Olave's School, St Thomas The Martyr C of E Primary School, Sawtry Community College, The Duchess's High School, Tideway School, Torfield School, Trinity C of E Primary School, Upper Poppelton School, Walton High School.

QCA and the Design Council would also like to thank the figures from public life who contributed their ideas about the value of each curriculum subject.